D1148856

Term-Time Trouble

Twink

Bimi

Pix

Sooze

Sili

Zena

Mariella

Lola

Glitterwings Academy

Book Six

Term-Time Trouble

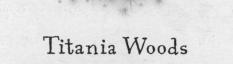

Titania Woods

Illustrated by Smiljana Coh

BLOOMSBURY

LONDON BERLIN NEW YORK

To Susan and Chuck

Bloomsbury Publishing, London, Berlin and New York

First published in Great Britain in 2008 by Bloomsbury Publishing Plc
36 Soho Square, London, W1D 3QY

This edition published in 2009

Text copyright © Lee Weatherly 2008
Illustrations copyright © Smiljana Coh 2008
The moral rights of the author and illustrator have been asserted

All rights reserved
No part of this publication may be reproduced or
transmitted by any means, electronic, mechanical, photocopying
or otherwise, without the prior permission of the publisher

A CIP catalogue record of this book is available from the British Library

ISBN 978 1 4088 0491 9

FSC

Mixed Sources

Product group from well-managed
forests and other controlled sources

Cert no. SGS - COC - 2061
www.fsc.org
© 1996 Forest Stewardship Council

Typeset by Dorchester Typesetting Group Ltd
Printed in Great Britain by Clays Ltd, St Ives Plc

1 3 5 7 9 10 8 6 4 2

www.glitterwingsacademy.co.uk

Chapter One

Drip! Drip!

Twink Flutterby groaned to herself as she flew along behind her parents. The rain had been drumming down all day, and showed no signs of stopping. What an awful start to the new term!

'Hold your umbrella higher!' called Twink's mother. 'Your wings are getting wet.'

'*Everything* is getting wet,' grumbled Twink, adjusting her rose-petal umbrella. Beads of silvery rain formed on its edge, racing off it like pearls. Twink shook it grumpily. 'I bet Glitterwings has

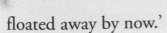

floated away by now.'

Her father laughed. 'Oh, I think you'll find it's still there. Your school has seen worse rain than this in its time!'

Twink's spirits lifted as Glitterwings Academy came into view. The massive oak tree sat calmly on its hill, its rich green leaves shiny with rain. Hundreds of tiny gold windows spiralled up its trunk, and a grand double door sat at its base, looking bright and welcoming despite the dampness.

For a change, though, there were no clusters of young fairies buzzing about the tree – it was far too wet for them! Instead, an oak-leaf pavilion had been set up on the front lawn for the returning students. Twink and her parents swooped inside it and landed thankfully on the dry grass. Everywhere Twink looked there were soggy fairies!

'Aren't you going to tell us how beautiful Glitterwings is in the summertime?' Twink's father teased her mother as the rain pattered loudly overhead. Twink's mother had gone to Glitterwings herself as a young fairy, and tended to wax nostalgic whenever she saw the school again.

She laughed. 'Well, it is — but I do like it better in the sunshine!' she admitted.

Looking around, Twink caught sight of a thin fairy with light blue wings called Lola, standing with her mother. Lola was a second-year fairy like Twink, and the two of them had been in the same branch since Twink's first term.

Even so, Twink hesitated when she saw Lola. Nobody really liked the washed-out little fairy very much — she was the only friend of a perfectly horrid fairy called Mariella, and nobody in their right wings could like Mariella!

'Isn't that girl in your branch?' said Twink's mother, noticing her too.

Twink nodded reluctantly. 'Yes . . . but . . .'

'Poor thing, she looks so sad!' said Twink's mother. 'Why don't you go and say hello to her while we register you with Miss Sparkle?'

Lola, sad? The thought had never occurred to Twink, but looking at Lola now, she could see what her mother meant. Lola's blonde hair looked damp and stringy, and her mouth was turned down in an unhappy grimace.

'All right,' said Twink doubtfully.

'Good girl,' said her dad. His expression told her that he understood her dilemma, and was proud of her for doing the right thing.

Warmed by the thought, Twink smoothed back her pink hair and flitted through the crowd towards Lola. She slowed down as she drew near, becoming uncomfortably aware that an argument was taking place between Lola and her mother.

'Mum, you're not being fair!' Lola beat her wings fretfully. 'I've told you over and over –'

'You'll do as I say,' said Lola's mother, a large fairy with powerful-looking wings and a firm mouth. 'I don't want to discuss it again, and that's that!'

'But you're not even listening!' Lola looked close to tears. 'I *hate* it, don't you see? I gave it a chance like you said, but –'

'Nonsense!' boomed Lola's mother. 'Of course you don't hate it. Now, have a good term, and write every week. And I expect much better reports from

your teachers this term!'

Lola stared down at the ground. 'Yes, Mother,' she mumbled.

Twink watched as Lola's mother flapped away, wondering what the argument had been about. Poor Lola! How awful to have a mother who bouldered right over you like that.

She edged forward. 'Hi, Lola.'

Lola's head jerked up. Hastily, she drew a hand over her eyes. 'Oh. Hi.'

Twink swallowed, not at all sure what to say. It wasn't as if she and Lola ever spoke to each other! 'Did you . . . um . . . have good hols?'

'Yeah, glimmery,' said Lola sourly. 'How about you?'

'Great.' Twink's voice sounded weak, even to her own ears. She *had* had great hols, but now didn't seem the time to go into the details. She struggled to think of something else to say.

'*There* you are, Lola – I've been looking every-where for you!' A fairy with silvery-green hair and pale green wings landed beside them and tucked her

arm through Lola's. She narrowed her eyes at Twink. 'Hello.'

'Hi, Mariella,' said Twink wearily. She and Mariella had reached a truce of sorts last term, as they both played on the school's Fledge team. Even so, she couldn't truthfully say that she liked the pointy-faced fairy very much.

The feeling was clearly mutual. Lifting her nose in the air, Mariella tugged at Lola's arm. 'Come on, Lo, let's go and catch up. I hardly heard from you all hols!'

Lola hesitated. 'Yes, but I've just got here. I need

to go to Peony Branch, and –'

'I've already saved our old beds for us,' said Mariella impatiently. 'Come *on*.'

She dragged Lola away through the crowd. Watching them go, it struck Twink that Lola hadn't seemed very pleased to see Mariella.

How strange – they're supposed to be best friends! she thought in surprise. Maybe they'd had a row.

Then she forgot all about Lola as a familiar voice called her name. Whirling about, Twink saw her own best friend, Bimi Bluebell, flying towards her. The two fairies embraced with shrieks of delight.

'It's so good to see you!' cried Twink.

'I know!' Bimi's pretty face was flushed with excitement.

If Bimi weren't so nice, Twink often thought she'd be too shy to even speak to her – for Bimi was easily the prettiest fairy in the school, with her dark blue hair and shimmering gold and silver wings. But Bimi was the best friend in the world, and not stuck-up in the least.

'Guess what?' Bimi fluttered her wings madly,

almost lifting off the ground. 'Mum was talking to Miss Shimmery, and it's official – we're going to have a term of Sparkle Art!'

'Oh, hurrah!' cried Twink. She had hoped for ages that the school would find a Sparkle Art teacher. Fairies loved anything that sparkled, and creating works of *art* that sparkled sounded like excellent fun!

Just then Twink saw her mother waving at her from across the pavilion. She tugged Bimi's hand. 'Come on, let's say goodbye to my parents before they leave.'

The two friends flitted through the crowd arm in arm, giggling as they tried to avoid bumping into other fairies. Twink sighed happily. Rain or not, she could tell already that it was going to be a perfectly glimmery term!

After her parents had left, Twink and Bimi took their bags and darted out into the rain, squealing as they shot through the open double doors at the base of the oak tree.

The inside of Glitterwings Academy was a high, golden tower that stretched up as far as the eye could see, with branches shooting off in all directions. Fairies darted in and out of the branches, laughing and calling to each other. Twink smiled. Oh, it was glimmery to be back! No matter how many terms she'd spent at Glitterwings, it still looked magical to her.

'You're such a slow-worm!' laughed Bimi, nudging her with her wing. 'Hurry, let's get to Peony Branch – we want the same beds as last term, don't we?'

The two fairies leapt into the air. Spiralling quickly up the trunk, they passed dozens of sleeping branches, along with empty classrooms filled with red and white spotted mushroom seats. Finally, near the top of the tree, they came to a branch with an upside-down peony hanging over it.

'Good old Peony Branch!' said Twink, pushing open the door.

A curving branch lined with soft mossy beds met her eyes. Over each bed hung a sweet-smelling peony, and cosy bark cabinets were tucked away here and there. Normally sunshine spilled into the branch, but today there were only grey, streaky shadows as the rain pattered down the arched windows.

Twink's face fell. Her old bed had already been taken! An unfamiliar fairy with spiky green hair sat on it, reading a petal mag.

'Who's that?' whispered Bimi.

'I don't know,' Twink murmured back. They had been with the same group of fairies since they started school – were they to have a new girl now?

A clever red-haired fairy called Pix flitted over to

them. 'We tried to save your usual beds for you two,' she said, 'but *she* wouldn't move!' She gave the fairy with green hair a hard stare. The fairy flipped a page of her petal mag without even glancing up.

Twink and Bimi looked at each other in disappointment. They had loved those two beds on the end last term – it was lovely and private off to the side, plus there was an extra cupboard.

Finally Twink shrugged. 'Well . . . she got here first, I suppose.'

Bimi nodded with a sigh. 'We can take those two beds in the middle.'

'It's funny that she wouldn't move, isn't it?' whispered Twink as they started to unpack. She knew that if she'd been a fairy in a new school, she'd have wanted the other fairies to like her. Refusing to give up her bed to girls who had been there for ages wasn't a good way to go about it.

Overhearing her, a yellow-haired fairy called Zena flitted over. 'She's called Jax, and she's *awful*,' she hissed, flapping her orange wings. 'I don't know what we've done wrong to get saddled with *her*.

When we already have Mariella and Lola, too!'

'What's so awful about her?' whispered Bimi, her blue eyes wide.

Zena made a face. 'Just try talking to her. Everything about Glitterwings is rubbish, according to her!'

Twink peered over her shoulder at Jax. The green-haired fairy sat scowling at her petal mag. Everything about her said *Keep away – I'm not interested!*

Should Twink say something to her? She bit her lip, unsure whether to bother if she was going to be rebuffed. Before she could decide, a fairy with lavender hair and pink wings burst into the branch.

'Hello, everybody!' she called, dropping her oak-leaf bag on the floor. Sweeping her long hair back with both hands, she wrung it out dramatically. 'Ugh! This awful rain!'

Sooze! Twink looked up with an expectant grin as the other fairies chorused hellos. Sili, an excitable fairy with silver hair, caught Sooze up in a tight hug.

'Oh, I'm so glad you're here!' she cried. 'It's been so boring without you!'

Sooze laughed. 'Already? The new term's hardly

started.' She threw herself on to the last unoccupied mossy bed, bouncing up and down. 'Hello, Opposite!' she called across to Twink.

Twink smiled at the nickname. She had pink hair and lavender wings – the exact *opposite* of Sooze. 'Hi, Sooze!' she called back. 'Did you have good hols?'

Sooze nodded. 'Brilliant! And guess what?' She glanced around impishly at the others. 'I've already had a super-glimmery idea about how we can liven things up around here!'

Sili squealed and clasped her hands together. 'Ooh, *have* you? Tell us!'

Sooze stopped bouncing and lowered her voice. 'Well, you know Rona, that purple-haired fairy in Jasmine Branch?' The others nodded. Jasmine Branch was a third-year branch, and Rona a fairy who thought she was a bit superior to everyone else.

'Well, I accidentally crashed into her on my way in, and she got her wings in a twist over it – silly flea, it's not like I did it on purpose! Then she and some of her Jasmine friends started going on. They

said that Peony Branch is the worst branch in the
school, and that we're all a bunch of clumsy wasp
brains!'

The fairies exchanged indignant glances. *How
dare they!* thought Twink. Peony Branch was
perfectly glimmery. Everyone knew that!

'Well, of course I told them what I thought of
Jasmine Branch after that!' Sooze grinned. 'But I
reckon we still need to get back at them properly.
And I know just the way to do it!'

'A prank, you mean?' asked Sili eagerly as the

fairies drew closer.

'Of course!' Sooze shot Twink a look, her violet eyes sparkling. 'Will you help me, Opposite? I couldn't do it without you!'

A tingle of excitement swept through Twink. She knew Bimi wouldn't approve – her best friend thought Sooze was unreliable, and deep down, Twink knew she had a point. But how could she possibly refuse? It sounded too glimmery for words!

'Yes, I'll help!' she decided, not meeting Bimi's eyes.

'Hurrah!' cried Sooze, shooting up into the air. 'We'll start planning right away – hang on, who's Miss Cheerful over there?' she demanded suddenly, catching sight of Jax.

Jax threw her petal mag down. 'I suppose you mean me,' she snapped. 'I'm called Jax – not that it's any of your business!'

Pix shook her head with a groan. 'Yes, and she seems to *always* be this charming. Don't fairies bother to be polite where you come from, Jax?'

'Why should I be polite?' demanded Jax furiously.

'I didn't ask to be sent to this rubbish school. It's just like all the rest — awful! So if you don't like the way I act, then don't talk to me!' She snatched up her petal mag again and buried herself in its pages.

'Well, lucky us,' said Sooze after a pause. 'I reckon we should do as Jax suggests, and leave her alone!'

The Great Branch was the largest branch in the school. Dozens of mossy tables were lined up and down its polished wooden floor, with a large, colourful flower hanging over each one for the different branches.

Twink and her friends sat at the Peony Branch table, watching as the rest of the school flitted in. Sooze caught Twink's eye as Jasmine Branch arrived. 'Ha!' she whispered. 'Look at them — the smug things!'

Twink had to agree that the Jasmine fairies looked rather smug. Rona and her friends had obviously spread the word. One of the Jasmine fairies smirked when she caught sight of Sooze, and mimed clumsy flying. The others giggled.

'Watch out!' called Rona over the noise of the Great Branch. 'We're only four tables away from Peony Branch – they might all crash into us on their way out. They haven't quite got the hang of flying yet, you know.'

Oh! Twink grimaced as the Jasmine fairies snorted with laughter. Sooze rolled her eyes. 'They won't be laughing long,' she whispered to the rest of the table. 'Just wait and see!'

Sili's large eyes grew even larger. 'What are you going to do to them, Sooze?'

Sooze shook her head. 'Sorry, but that's top secret – strictly between me and my Opposite.' She gave Twink a broad wink.

Twink tried to look as cool as Sooze, but her insides felt fizzy with excitement. There was something so thrilling about being Sooze's friend! Bimi, sitting next to her, said nothing, and Twink felt a pinch of guilt that she was being left out. She squeezed her best friend's hand, and Bimi gave her a small smile.

A hush fell over the Great Branch. Miss

Shimmery, the HeadFairy, lifted into the air from the raised platform at the front, her rainbow wings gleaming like prisms. The students turned and faced her expectantly.

'Welcome, all of you, to a new summer term at Glitterwings,' said Miss Shimmery in her low, strong voice. 'Though it's rather a damp one so far, I'm afraid!'

The Branch laughed.

Twink settled on to her mushroom as the

HeadFairy put on her sparkle specs and made the usual announcements – no fast flying in the school, uniforms required from tomorrow, and a special welcome to all new girls.

Miss Shimmery's white hair shone like a cloud as she smiled down at the Peony Branch table. 'Welcome to Glitterwings Academy, Jax. I know that your branchmates will do everything they can to make you feel at home.'

Jax slumped down on her mushroom, looking crosser than ever. Twink sighed. They'd have a hard time making *her* feel at home – unless Jax was as awful to her family as she was to everyone else!

'One final announcement.' Looking out at the school again, Miss Shimmery adjusted her sparkle specs firmly. 'I'm sure I don't have to remind you that I expect my students to be well behaved at all times. Any rule-breaking this term will be looked upon very sternly indeed – so please, save your energy for your schoolwork.'

Her gaze fell lightly on the Jasmine Branch table, and then moved to the Peony fairies for a moment before scanning the rest of the school. Twink gulped. It was as though Miss Shimmery had read their minds!

'Now then, I think it's time for a well-deserved meal.' Miss Shimmery clapped her hands as she drifted gracefully to the ground. 'Butterflies commence!'

A river of brightly coloured butterflies floated into the branch, carrying oak-leaf platters piled high with seed cakes and nectar. A butterfly with yellow wings served the Peony Branch table, its antennae waving gently.

Sooze took a seed cake and leaned towards Twink. 'Right, do you want to hear my plan? What I think we should do is –'

'Sooze, maybe we shouldn't,' said Twink worriedly. 'You heard what Miss Shimmery said.'

Sooze's mouth dropped open. 'But we can't just let Jasmine Branch get *away* with this. You saw them! We have to do something.'

Twink squirmed. 'I know – but –' She broke off, glancing across the table at Sili. The silver-haired fairy quickly made a show of talking to Zena, but Twink knew she was listening to every word – and that *she'd* be more than happy to do the prank with Sooze if Twink didn't.

'I'm not sure if you should, Twink,' put in Bimi. 'I think Miss Shimmery meant what she said.'

'Oh, don't be such a wet leaf!' snapped Sooze. 'Come on, Twink, just one little prank. What harm can it do?'

Bimi's mouth tightened. 'Yes, but it won't stop at one, will it?' she pointed out. 'Because then *they'll* play a prank, too, and then you'll play another one, and then –'

Twink felt a rush of irritation towards Bimi. She sounded like Twink's mother! And in front of the whole table, too. 'All right,' she said, before she could change her mind. 'I guess just one prank can't hurt.' She heard Bimi sigh, and hastened to add, 'But that's really all, Sooze! We don't want to get into trouble.'

'One prank. That's all,' said Sooze solemnly. 'Cross my wings and hope to fly!'

Chapter Two

Two weeks later, Twink thought that she really should have known Bimi would be right. For of course the pranks hadn't stopped at just one. She'd been an idiot to ever suppose they would!

First Twink and Sooze had cast a fairy dust spell on Jasmine Branch's oak-leaf caps, so that they wouldn't come off no matter how hard the fairies tugged. Then a few of the Jasmine fairies had retaliated by turning Peony Branch's pixie boots into gnats that had buzzed all over the branch, refusing to be caught.

Other pranks had followed, each more inventive than the last. The rivalry between the branches became more good-natured as it went on, with each striving to play the most outrageous prank yet. Neither branch would have dreamt of giving the other away – they were having far too much fun!

It was becoming difficult to think of excuses, though. '*What* is the meaning of this?' Mrs Hover, the matron, had demanded just that morning, propping her hands on her ample hips. 'Where are all your thistle combs?'

The Peony fairies had quickly stifled their giggles at the sight of the snail shells sitting on their bedside mushrooms. How had the Jasmine fairies managed *that*?

'There was a bad batch of fairy dust in class yesterday!' said Sooze, her eyes wide and innocent. 'I must have brought some of it back with me without realising it, and it got loose. Can you change them back, Hovey?'

Mrs Hover had done so, grumbling to herself as the fairies exchanged relieved glances. They had got away with it, thought Twink – but how much longer could they expect to? They were sure to get caught soon. But they couldn't stop now; Jasmine Branch was one up on them!

'Shh!' hissed Sooze over her shoulder. 'We're almost there!'

The great tree was dark and still, its branches filled with sleeping fairies. Despite her misgivings, Twink's spine tingled as she and Sooze glided silently downwards in their nightclothes.

Sooze landed on a ledge beside a closed door. Twink touched down at her side, fluttering her wings. The cluster of white jasmine blossoms that hung over the door swayed slightly.

'Ready?' whispered Sooze.

Twink nodded. 'But Sooze, this really does have to be the last one – agreed?'

'Of course!' said Sooze impatiently. 'Now let's get on with it.' Reaching into her pocket, she carefully drew out some blue powder. 'Do you have the fairy dust?'

Twink fumbled at a small pouch on her hip. Yes, the fairy dust that she had sneaked out of class that afternoon was still there. It sparkled as she drew out a pink and gold handful.

She cupped the fairy dust in her palms. Sooze poured the blue powder on to it and stirred it about with her finger. Immediately, the pink and gold dust changed to a bright, shimmering blue that seemed to dance in the moonlight.

'What now?' Twink whispered.

Sooze frowned, tapping her wings together. 'Um . . . I'm trying to remember the words.'

'You haven't forgotten them!' cried Twink.

'No, I remember. Now, concentrate!' Shutting her eyes, Sooze put her hands over Twink's and chanted, *'Fairy dust and blueberry flakes, turn them blue before they wake!'*

Sooze eased open the door and motioned furiously. Twink flung the dust into the branch. She had a fleeting glimpse of a dark room with a cloud of sparkling blue dust drifting through it, and then Sooze popped the door shut again. 'Come on, let's get out of here!'

The two fairies leapt upwards, winging their way back to Peony Branch. A wild giggle welled up inside Twink. Playing pranks *was* great fun, there was no denying it. And Jasmine Branch had quite a surprise in store for them tomorrow!

It was even better than Twink had expected. When the Jasmine fairies flew into the Great Branch for breakfast the next morning, there was first a surprised murmur – and then peals of delighted laughter echoed across the Branch. The school twisted on their mushrooms, straining to see.

The Peony Branch table spluttered with mirth as they caught sight of the sheepish fairies. 'Oh, Sooze!' cried Sili, clapping her hands over her mouth. 'You and Twink are *brilliant*! Look at them!'

'That – is *so* glimmery.' Zena wiped tears of laughter from her eyes.

Pix shook her head in admiration. 'How did you ever think of it, Sooze?'

Sooze shrugged modestly. 'I don't know. I just thought they'd look better with blue noses, that's all.' She smiled at Twink. 'Right, Opposite?'

'Right!' said Twink. Oh, she had never seen anything so funny! The Jasmine Branch fairies all sat red-cheeked at their table, trying desperately to pretend that nothing was out of the ordinary . . . but each and every one of them had a bright blue nose!

'Well, I think it's stupid,' snapped Mariella, flipping back her silvery-green hair. 'And if we all get into trouble for it, it'll be *your* fault, Sooze.'

'But at least you know better now than to run off

and tell on us, don't you, Mosquito Nose?' pointed out Sooze with a wicked grin. And it was true that once Mariella would have done exactly that, but she had learned her lesson too many times to be tempted now.

The pointy-faced fairy glared at Sooze, and then turned away with a haughty sniff to whisper in Lola's ear. Lola smiled, but didn't look very happy. And Jax, sitting alone at the end of the table, had a glower on her face that was practically set in stone.

Twink noticed that Bimi hadn't said anything, either. She leaned towards her friend. 'Bimi, you *do* think it's funny, don't you?' she whispered.

Bimi smiled, but her eyes were troubled. 'Of course!' she whispered back. 'But Twink, it's just going to keep on and on, and you know that the two of you are bound to get caught soon –'

'Your attention, please!' announced a loud voice. Looking up, Twink saw with alarm that Miss Shimmery was hovering above the platform . . . and that she was looking directly at them.

'The Jasmine Branch fairies appear to have

something wrong with their noses,' observed Miss Shimmery dryly. The school started to snigger again, but the expression on the HeadFairy's face stopped them. Silence fell over the Branch.

Miss Shimmery beat her wings together sternly. 'I have no doubt that if I ask them how their noses became blue they'll tell me they've encountered a bad batch of fairy dust – which, by a worrying coincidence, has also happened to the Peony Branch fairies several times over the last few weeks.'

Twink gulped. Oh dear! They obviously hadn't been as clever in fooling Mrs Hover as they had thought. She smoothed her hands anxiously over her peony-petal uniform.

'I am extremely concerned about this rogue fairy dust that's causing so many problems,' continued Miss Shimmery. 'Twink Flutterby, I should like to see you in my office directly after breakfast to discuss the matter.'

The HeadFairy floated serenely back down to the teachers' table. Twink felt the blood drain from her wings. *Her?* But what about Sooze?

Her friends obviously had no more idea what was going on than she did. They stared at her wordlessly, horror written on their faces. Bimi looked worried, but thankfully didn't say anything. Twink didn't think she could have borne to hear 'I told you so!' just then!

'Well, I suppose it was pretty easy to work out that there was a prank war going on,' said Pix finally. 'But Twink, why does she want to see *you*?'

Twink shook her head. 'I – I don't know.'

Oh, it wasn't fair that she should get into trouble if Sooze didn't! Yet how could she tell Miss Shimmery that without being a tell-tale? And what if Miss Shimmery told her parents? Twink's wings slumped miserably at the thought.

All at once Sooze leaned across the table and squeezed Twink's hand. 'Don't worry, Opposite,' she said. 'It's my fault, not yours – and I'll go along with you and tell her so!'

But when the two fairies flitted nervously into Miss Shimmery's office after breakfast, the HeadFairy shook her snowy-white head. 'Just you, Twink. Not Sooze as well.'

Sooze didn't move. 'But I need to explain! You see, it's not Twink's fault. I –'

A slight smile appeared on Miss Shimmery's face. 'Thank you, Sooze, but I'm aware that it's not entirely Twink's fault. Please go on to Fairy Dust class now.'

Sooze licked her lips. 'But –'

'Close the door as you leave.' There was no mistaking the firm tone in Miss Shimmery's voice. Sooze flew off reluctantly, looking over her shoulder.

Twink's wings felt icy as she stood alone on the ornate petal carpet. The last time she'd been in this office was three terms before, when she had befriended a wasp named Stripe. She had been certain then that she'd be expelled, and she didn't feel much braver now.

Miss Shimmery sat at her mushroom desk and folded her rainbow wings behind her back. 'Now then, Twink. It's quite obvious that there's a prank

war going on between your branch and Jasmine Branch.'

It didn't seem to be a question, but Twink nodded anyway. 'Yes, Miss Shimmery,' she mumbled. 'But – but it wasn't *completely* our fault. They –'

The HeadFairy cut her off with a wave of her wing. 'I'm not interested in who started it, or who's done what to whom. I don't mind a few good-natured pranks, but it's all got a bit silly now, and I've had enough. Mrs Hover says it's going to take half the morning to get those noses back to normal.'

Twink squirmed where she stood. Oh, *why* hadn't she listened to Bimi? 'Yes, Miss. We'll stop now,' she whispered.

Miss Shimmery considered her keenly. 'I know you will. Because I'm putting you in charge of Peony Branch.'

Twink's mouth fell open. 'You – you what?' she stammered.

'You're in charge,' repeated Miss Shimmery. Her voice was grave, but there was an unmistakable twinkle in her eye. 'You see, Twink, I think both the

Peony and the Jasmine fairies are old enough now to work this sort of thing out for themselves, without the school having to get involved. And just to make certain you do, I'm putting one fairy in charge of each of the branches. If there are any further problems that occur this term – and I mean *any* further problems – then that fairy will be directly responsible for them.'

Twink fell into a horror-struck silence. *She* was meant to be responsible for *Sooze*? But how on earth could she make Sooze do anything? The lavender-haired fairy did exactly what she wanted!

'But . . . why me?' she asked finally.

Miss Shimmery smiled. 'I have my reasons, but I think I'll let you find them out for yourself.'

'Oh,' said Twink blankly.

Miss Shimmery laughed and stood up. 'You can go now, Twink. But remember what I said. I don't want to hear another word about any trouble from Peony Branch. If anything comes up, I expect you to deal with it yourself!'

Chapter Three

'Really?' Sooze's eyes lit up. 'But that's glimmery! If *you're* in charge, that means we can get away with whatever we like! We can have midnight feasts every night! We can have flying pillow fights! We can –'

'Sooze, no!' cried Twink. They were sitting with the others in the second-year Common Branch, sprawled about the fire rocks – enchanted rocks that glowed warm in winter and cool in the heat of summer.

'Don't you see?' she went on. '*I'm* the one who'd get blamed. It's not fair.'

'That's right, Sooze,' said Pix. 'In fact, we'll have to be doubly good, just to make sure that Twink stays out of trouble. Right, everyone?' She glanced at Bimi, Sili and Zena, who all nodded seriously.

Sooze stared at them, aghast. '*Doubly* good? When Twink's in charge? Are you all mad?'

Twink saw Bimi start to say something and then stop, her face flushing angrily. Twink knew she was thinking how irresponsible Sooze was being – and for a change, Twink was beginning to see what she meant!

She took a deep breath and tried again. 'Sooze, look. If –'

'Well, we'll at *least* do one more prank, though? Right?' Sooze hopped up on to a fire rock, looking at Sili and Zena for agreement. They hesitated, glancing doubtfully at each other.

'No!' burst out Twink, flapping her wings. 'No more pranks. I mean it, Sooze.'

Sooze's eyebrows shot up, and Twink's heart sank. She usually went along with whatever Sooze said – what would her Opposite think of her now?

But finally Sooze gave a sulky shrug. 'Oh, all right, Great Leader. Anyway, we definitely won with the blue noses, didn't we?'

'Definitely!' agreed Twink in relief.

The next step was to talk to the Jasmine Branch leader, and this, too, proved easier than expected. Miss Shimmery had put a quiet, thoughtful fairy called Taya in charge, and she was just as eager as Twink to call an end to the mischief.

'I just wish that we'd had a chance to play one last prank on you,' she said cheerfully as she and Twink touched wings to seal their promise. 'We had a glimmery one!'

Twink grinned. 'It's just as well you didn't. Then *we* would have had to play one last prank on *you*.'

Bimi smiled broadly when Twink told her the news. 'Oh, well done you! I have to say, I'm glad it's all over with now.' The two fairies were flying to Dance class, enjoying the sun on their wings as they skimmed across the field to the ring of enchanted mushrooms near the wood.

'Me too,' admitted Twink, banking to avoid a ladybird flittering past. 'Like Miss Shimmery said, it all got a bit silly, I suppose – but still, I wonder why she put *me* in charge?'

Bimi looked surprised. 'Well, why not? You did a glimmery job!'

Twink laughed. 'You're mad! Anyway, I'm just glad there won't be any more trouble, now that the pranks are finished. Being in charge of Sooze isn't much fun!'

'Quickly, girls, quickly – everyone else is here!' Madame Brightfoot clapped her hands from the centre of the circle as Twink and Bimi touched down. Her dramatic purple hair was piled atop her head, and her silvery cobweb robe sparkled as she moved.

'Today we learn a new dance!' she announced. 'A very, very special dance.'

The fairies all held their breath, wondering what the new dance would be. Madame drew herself up regally and announced, 'Today . . . we shall communicate with the earthworms!'

Oh. Twink's wings sagged in disappointment as the Peony Branch fairies grimaced at each other. Communicating with earthworms didn't sound very exciting!

'Ooh, glimmery,' whispered Sooze. 'We can hear about how thrilling it is to tunnel around in the dirt.'

Madame scowled as a giggle swept through the class. 'Enough! Petal position, quickly.'

As the fairies moved into a circle and clasped hands, Madame flitted to the centre and patted her hair into place. 'You must listen hard during this dance – the worms will sound very faint at first. You might hear the thoughts of the fairies on either side of you as well, but ignore them. Concentrate on the worms!'

Twink glanced curiously at Jax, who stood on her

right. The spiky-haired fairy's usual scowl became even more pronounced at Madame's words. She didn't look pleased at the idea of anyone reading *her* thoughts.

Just then a slight commotion caught Twink's attention. Across the circle, Lola had left Mariella's side, slipping in between Pix and Zena.

'Lola, where are you going?' hissed Mariella.

Lola's cheeks were rose-petal red. 'I . . . I just felt like a change, that's all.'

Mariella gaped at her. 'But you always stand beside me!'

Lola looked at the ground. 'I know, but . . .' Her voice trailed off, but she stayed where she was. Mariella's eyes narrowed.

'Hush, we are starting!' called Madame, clapping her hands. 'Wings touching, everyone.'

As Twink opened her wings so that they touched Bimi's wingtips on her left and Jax's on her right, she thought that she'd seldom seen Mariella look more incensed. Fancy Lola standing up to her!

'And we begin! Twirl in place! Tiptoe left! Tiptoe

right!' Madame hovered in the centre of the circle as the fairies followed her movements. 'Concentrate, concentrate! Listen for the earthworms!'

As Twink danced she became aware of Bimi's thoughts, and she smiled. They were so . . . Bimi-like! Warm and friendly, and slightly worried that she wasn't going to get the dance right.

Then Twink gasped as a wave of sadness swept through her. *I don't want to be here*, whispered a dejected voice in her mind. *I want to go home.*

Twink stared at Jax as she realised she was hearing the spiky-haired fairy's thoughts. Jax made a ferocious grimace and looked pointedly away.

Twink's own thoughts spun in confusion. Was *that* why Jax was so horrible and prickly to everyone – because she was homesick? She felt a rush of shame that she had ignored Jax so thoroughly. Maybe she'd like a friend, even if she pretended otherwise.

'That's enough,' announced Madame finally. She drifted back down to the ground, beaming happily. 'Did you all hear the worms?'

Twink hastily nodded with the others, though she had forgotten even to listen for them. From the bored expressions on her classmates' faces, she hadn't missed much!

Once class was over, Twink hurried to catch up with the new girl as they all flew back to Glitterwings. 'Jax, wait!' she called, putting on a burst of speed.

Jax spun about in midair, glaring at Twink. 'What?' she snapped. Her green hair looked like a spiky explosion.

Twink gulped, suddenly unsure whether this was a good idea. 'I just wanted to say . . . I mean . . . I'm sorry you're so sad,' she finished lamely.

Jax scowled at her. '*Sad?* Who said I'm sad?'

'Um . . . well, the dance – I sort of heard . . .' Twink stopped. Jax looked as if she might explode with fury.

'You're mad!' she snarled, clenching her fists. 'I'm not *sad* – why should I be?'

Twink licked her lips, wishing she hadn't said anything. 'I'm not sure, but it sounded like –'

'Oh! This is the worst school I've ever been in!' burst out Jax. 'For your information, I'm not sad, I'm *cross* — cross that I have to be here with all of you pathetic wasp brains!' She jetted off in an angry green flash. A bee darted out of her way with an alarmed buzz.

Twink sighed. Well, *that* had gone well. Next time, she'd keep her mouth shut!

At the end of classes every day, second-year students were expected to do an hour's study in the Common Branch — though this often consisted of fairies sitting on their mushroom desks, legs swinging as they laughed and chatted! With her petal bag over her shoulder, Twink skimmed up the trunk to begin the study time, thinking idly about her Flower Power homework.

'*Best* friends don't have secrets, Lola! What are you hiding from me?' The voice was low and threatening.

Peering over her shoulder, Twink saw Mariella and Lola flying nearby. Lola gulped. 'Nothing! I told you, I just fancied a change.'

Mariella glowered when she saw Twink. 'Well, never mind!' she snapped, tossing her hair back. 'I've got to go to my stupid Creature Kindness session now – but we'll talk about this later, Lola.'

She skimmed away down the trunk, leaving the thin little fairy looking shaken. Twink remembered that Mariella had fallen behind in her studies the previous term, and was having to do extra Creature Kindness sessions to catch up.

Adjusting the strap of her petal bag, Twink shook her head in bewilderment. 'Lola, why do you let her talk to you like that? You should stand up to her more – like you did today in Dance class!'

Lola ducked her head down. 'Oh, I don't know . . . she's not so bad, really,' she mumbled, and flew quickly off towards the Common Branch.

Twink stared after her for a moment, and then shrugged. It didn't make any sense to her why Lola would put up with such behaviour, but Lola's friends were her own business. If she was happy to put up with being bossed around by Mariella, then that was up to her!

After afternoon study, Twink and the others flew back to Peony Branch in a long, straggling line. 'Hurrah! Half an hour of free time!' Twink did a midair flip, and Bimi grinned at her.

'I've got a new petal mag, if you'd like to read it,' she offered.

'Ooh, glimmery!' said Twink. 'Yes, please!'

But as the two friends flitted into Peony Branch, Twink stopped short, all thoughts of the petal mag forgotten. She gaped as she tried to take in what she was seeing.

'Twink, what's – oh!' Bimi dropped her bag as she clapped her hands over her mouth.

'I don't believe it!' shrieked Sooze, skimming in just behind them. 'I thought there was a truce!'

'There is!' gasped Twink. 'Taya *promised* me –' She broke off, fluttering her wings in agitation. Maybe Taya had promised, but it was clear that the Jasmine Branch fairies hadn't been able to resist just one more prank.

The other fairies started to arrive just then, their eyes widening as they took in the scene before them.

'That's . . . sort of creepy,' whispered Sili.

Looking again, Twink thought that she agreed with her. Every single peony that hung over their beds had been shorn of its petals. They lay on the mossy beds below in forlorn pink piles.

'It's not creepy, it's *hideous*,' raged Sooze. She punched her fist into her palm. 'Ooh, those Jasmine Branch fairies! Well, they'll get what's coming to them. I've got a prank up my wing they'll *never* expect, and –'

'Sooze, no!' cried Twink. 'We can't start up the pranks again.'

Sooze glared at her. 'Why not? They did!'

'Yes, but . . .' Twink hesitated, conscious of everyone watching her. 'I want to talk to Taya,' she said finally.

'*Talk* to her?' scoffed Sooze, folding her arms across her chest. 'What for?'

'Just to see what she says.' Twink tried to sound more confident than she felt.

Pix nodded, looking worried. 'I think it's a good idea. There's something a bit strange about this. Their pranks have always been a good laugh – nothing like *this*.'

Twink saw what she meant. There was really nothing funny about this prank at all – their flowers looked so sad and bare without their petals. Lola's had been snapped clean off at the stem.

'So what are we meant to do now, Great Leader?' said Sooze drily, raising a lavender eyebrow.

Twink bit back a retort. 'Pix, why don't you see if

you can find a spell to put things right again, while the rest of you start tidying? I'll go and talk to Taya.'

She flew from the branch before Sooze could say anything else. Her wings felt like they were on fire. Oh, *why* had Miss Shimmery put her in charge? It was no fun at all!

Taya looked appalled when Twink described the state of their peonies. 'Really? Wasps, that's awful! No, it wasn't us – we've got a truce, remember?'

The two fairies were in the library, hovering near the top of the shelves as Taya searched for a book. 'Are you sure?' asked Twink. 'Maybe someone in your branch did it without you knowing.'

Taya shook her head firmly. 'We wouldn't go back on a promise, Twink – even though that blue-nose trick *was* unbelievably cheeky!' She shot Twink a grin, and Twink smiled back despite her worry. She believed Taya – the fairy gave no sign at all that she wasn't telling the truth.

But then what did that mean? Who had destroyed their flowers?

Taya flipped through a petal book and then slid it back on to the shelf. 'Maybe it wasn't a prank at all,' she suggested. 'Maybe the long-life spell on your peonies just wore off.'

'Maybe,' said Twink doubtfully, thinking of how some of the petals had been torn up and flung about the branch.

'Or maybe some other branch did it,' said Taya. 'Sooze isn't exactly careful about what she says, you know! She could have annoyed someone else, who decided to get back at you.'

Twink nodded slowly as the sunset angled in through the long library windows. 'You're probably right,' she decided. 'I'll ask Sooze if she can remember anything. And meanwhile, I just hope it doesn't happen again!'

Chapter Four

But the pranks *did* keep happening. Over the next few days, Peony Branch found itself the victim of several more pieces of mischief, each nastier than the last.

Sooze insisted that she hadn't said anything that might have annoyed one of the other branches. 'Everything isn't always *my* fault, you know,' she said crossly, helping herself to a seed cake at lunch one afternoon. 'I haven't done a thing!'

'Besides, who would do such awful things just to get back at Sooze?' put in Bimi anxiously. 'I'm really getting nervous, Twink!'

'Me too,' said Zena. The tall fairy's face was drawn. 'I think we need to go to Miss Shimmery.'

Twink hesitated. So far they had managed to mend everything themselves, but it was getting harder and harder to hide the episodes from Mrs Hover. How on earth were they supposed to explain torn homework all over their floor, or red berry paint splashed across their beds?

She bit glumly into a seed cake, hardly tasting it. She knew that the situation was becoming quite serious, yet Miss Shimmery had been adamant – Twink was meant to deal with any problems on her own.

'Let's wait just a bit longer,' she said. 'We *must* be able to work out who's doing it, if we just put our wings together.'

Sili shivered. 'All I know is, someone really has it in for us! I'm getting scared to even go back to our branch.'

The others murmured in agreement. Twink glanced over her shoulder at all the tables of laughing, chattering fairies. It was dreadful to think that someone in the school hated them so much. But *why*?

'Come on, let's think!' she repeated urgently, clapping her wings together. 'Who might be doing this? Pix, don't *you* have any idea?'

There was a pause. 'I might have,' said Pix finally. 'But I'm not going to say anything just yet.'

The Peony Branch table erupted in excited whispers. 'Who, Pix?' demanded Sooze, leaning forward.

Pix shook her head. 'I'm not going to say. Not until I'm certain.'

Sitting at the end of the table, Lola looked quite pale. Twink felt a rush of sympathy for her. She was such a nervous little fairy anyway – this must be awful for her.

Sooze huffed out an irritated breath. 'Oh, great! So we have to wait until one of us is . . . is *attacked* by some deranged fairy before you'll do anything?'

'Of course not,' said Pix irritably. 'But this is serious, Sooze. I can't accuse someone without a bit more proof.'

Mariella tossed her head. 'Well, *I* think it's ridiculous!' she snapped. 'We can't just let someone destroy our branch – we've got to *do* something.'

'Hang on,' said Sooze, her violet eyes suddenly wide in pretend alarm. 'Are we actually agreeing with each other, Mosquito Nose? Wasps, things *must* be bad!'

The tension at the table lessened as everyone laughed.

'I – I think we should tell Miss Shimmery!' burst out Lola. The others stopped talking and stared at her. Lola hardly ever said a word, unless she was backing up Mariella.

Lola's cheeks blazed, but she kept on. 'I mean – I mean, maybe our parents should know about this. It's *dangerous*.'

'What, and get Twink into trouble?' demanded Pix. 'Lola, we can't – you know what Miss Shimmery said. We've got to try to solve it ourselves first.'

Lola's face burned even redder. 'Oh. I – I just thought . . .' She stopped, staring down at the table.

'What about *you*, Jax?' said Sooze suddenly.

Everyone looked curiously at the spiky-haired fairy. She hadn't said a word all through the conversation, thought Twink – but then, you could count on one wing the number of times that she'd joined in with them since she'd arrived.

Jax stopped chewing her seed cake and scowled. 'What *about* me?'

Sooze met her gaze coolly. 'Has anything like this ever happened at one of your other schools?'

Jax's green eyebrows drew together. 'No. Should it have?'

'Who knows?' said Sooze, lifting a wing. 'This sort of thing is completely new to *us*.'

Jax looked thunderous, but didn't reply. Twink glanced uneasily from one to the other, wondering if she should say anything. Before she could decide, the school's butterflies fluttered in to clear the tables, their wings dipping gracefully in the air.

'What was *that* about?' Twink whispered to Sooze as the fairies flitted from the Branch.

Sooze shrugged. 'Just working on a theory of my own, that's all.'

Sparkle Art class was a welcome distraction from Twink's problems. Mr Prism, a tall fairy with bright blue wings and a vivid shock of crimson hair, turned out to be a wonderful teacher – nothing at all like nervous Mr Woodleaf, who taught Creature Kindness and seemed terrified of them!

'Welcome!' cried Mr Prism that afternoon, grinning widely as the Peony Branch fairies flew into his branch. 'Are we all ready to create some super-spectacular artwork? Excellent! Take your seats, girls, take your seats.'

'I love this class!' whispered Bimi to Twink. She gave a little bounce as they sat perched on their spotted mushrooms.

'Me too!' Twink whispered back. Sparkle Art was just as much fun as she'd imagined: they used fairy dust mixed with paint to create glittering works of art, often getting delightfully messy in the process!

She watched eagerly as Mr Prism set up a piece of white birch bark at the front of the branch. 'Today we're going to do self-portraits,' he announced, bringing out the fairy-dust paint from a bark cupboard. Rainbow-coloured sparks fizzed from the acorn pots.

Twink and Bimi exchanged an excited look. Self-portraits sounded glimmery!

Mr Prism ran a hand through his crimson hair. 'Now, then! In Sparkle Art, you *think* what you want to draw, and the fairy dust does the work for you – right?'

Twink nodded with the others.

'But no two paintings are ever the same, because

everything depends on *you* – your mood, your thoughts, your personality! Paint a mouse,' Mr Prism commanded the paints.

Immediately, brown and black paint leapt from the pots in a glittering stream, landing on the white bark with little *plopping* noises. A mouse started to form – but it was like no mouse Twink had ever seen! Its teeth were long and sinister, and its eyes glared out at them from the painting.

The class gasped in surprise. Mr Prism grinned apologetically. 'I was scared by a mouse in acorn school,' he explained. 'Never liked 'em since! But if one of *you* lot painted a mouse, I bet it would come out all cute and cuddly.'

Twink smiled, knowing he was right. Brownie, her family's own beloved mouse, had been her friend since she was a baby!

'So Sparkle Art is all about how *you* feel about what you're painting,' continued Mr Prism, wiping the mouse away with a damp piece of moss. 'And when you're doing self-portraits, that gets very interesting indeed!'

'What do you mean, sir?' asked Pix.

'Watch!' Mr Prism put his hands behind his back and said, 'Paint a portrait of Thaddeus Prism, Sparkle Art teacher extraordinaire!'

A rainbow stream of colours sprang from the pots. Twink craned to see as an image started to form.

The class had sniggered at the name 'Thaddeus' – and now the sniggers turned to howls of laughter. The painting showed an impossibly handsome fairy, with a brilliant smile and gleaming wings.

'What?' said Mr Prism, feigning hurt. 'Don't you think it's a good likeness?' He struck a heroic pose, jutting his chin out. 'It looks just like me!'

When the laughter had died down, Mr Prism said, 'You see, Sparkle Art self-portraits are how *you* see yourself, not how you really are! We'll be doing several over the next few weeks. You'll be surprised how your different moods can change your portrait!' He started passing out rolls of birch bark and paint pots.

'I'm a bit nervous!' whispered Bimi.

Adjusting her bark on the twiggy easel that sat in

Mr Prism

front of her, Twink realised that she was, too. What sort of fairy would her painting show?

'Ready?' said Mr Prism. 'Right, then! Off you go!'

Twink cleared her throat. 'Um . . . paint Twink Flutterby,' she said to her acorn pots. Immediately, pink and lavender paint leapt out, arranging itself on the birch bark in delicate swirls and hops.

'Oh!' cried Twink as the painting took shape. Her wings felt hot with embarrassment. The fairy staring back at her had an anxious smile on her face and a giant oak-leaf badge on her chest: *Peony Branch Head.*

Bimi burst out laughing when she saw it. 'Oh, Twink, you poor thing! You look so *worried.*'

Twink giggled despite herself. Bimi was right. She looked like the ceiling was about to fall in on her!

Mr Prism came across. 'Very interesting,' he said, tapping his chin with a smile. 'Bimi, how did you do?'

Bimi's cheeks blazed. 'Oh – all right, I guess. Only I look too pretty.'

Twink leaned across to see Bimi's portrait. A rather plain fairy with dull blue hair and gaudily bright wings looked back at her.

'But that's nothing like you!' she said in surprise, looking at Bimi's midnight-blue hair, and the gracefully swirling patterns on her wings. 'You're *much* prettier than that.'

The other fairies' portraits were even funnier. Pix's showed a serious-looking fairy surrounded by looming piles of books, while the fairy in Mariella's painting had a sweet, pleasant expression – and a much shorter nose than in real life.

'I don't see what's so funny,' complained Mariella when the other girls howled.

'No, you wouldn't,' sniggered Sooze. Oddly enough, thought Twink, Sooze's portrait was the only one that had come out halfway normal.

Mariella tossed her hair. 'Let's see yours, Lola,' she commanded. 'I bet that's *really* something to laugh at.'

Lola's face paled. 'Oh – no, it's not that funny, really.'

She hastily wiped her birch bark clean before anyone could see. Mariella scowled.

'What about *your* portrait, Jax?' asked Sooze, fluttering her wings innocently. 'I bet it's really glimmery.'

'None of your business,' snapped the spiky-haired fairy. Taking her birch bark off her easel, she rolled it up and tucked it away in her petal bag. She stared at the rest of the class defiantly, daring them to say anything.

'Ooh, that must be a *really* interesting one,' grinned Sooze.

'No one has to share who doesn't want to,' said Mr Prism. 'That's enough for today, girls. We'll have another crack at self-portraits next time.'

What a funny lesson! thought Twink as she put her things away. Who would have thought there could be so many different ways for fairies to see themselves?

As the magpie's call rang through the school, Jax jetted off, the first to leave the branch. Twink glanced after her, curious despite herself.

And what *had* Jax's portrait been like?

That afternoon in the Common Branch, Twink flitted to her favourite mushroom desk and started setting out her things – a work petal for Fairy Dust class, a mustard seed for Flower Power, her pen . . . hang on, where was her pen?

'I've forgotten my snail-trail pen!' she complained, peering into the depths of her pink petal bag. 'I must have dropped it up in the branch when I popped in to comb my hair.'

Bimi looked up from her mustard seed, her blue eyebrows drawn together with the effort to make it sprout. 'Would you like to borrow mine?'

Twink shook her head. She was very attached to her pen; it was the one Bimi had given her for her birthday last year. 'No, it'll just take me a wing beat to get it. I'll be back in a minute!'

Skimming out of the door, Twink flew upwards, darting quickly around chattering clusters of fairies. She looked wistfully at a pair of upper-year fairies wearing sparkly shorts and bright petal waistcoats.

How glimmery to get to wear your own clothes after lessons each day – and what a shame that you had to wait until you were practically elderly to do so.

Reaching Peony Branch, Twink landed with a hop on its ledge and skipped inside. 'Oh!' she cried, pulling up short. 'Lola, what are *you* doing here?'

The thin little fairy spun about to face her, wide-eyed. 'I – I forgot something,' she stammered. 'So I came back to get it, but – but oh, Twink, look!' she wailed. She pointed to her mossy bed.

Twink gulped. Lola's petal duvet had been ripped to bits. It hung in limp, tattered ribbons from her bed, as though it had been attacked with a rose thorn.

'Someone must really hate me,' sobbed Lola. Her wings shook as she covered her face with her hands. 'No one else's duvet was even touched! But why me? What have I done wrong?'

Twink rubbed her lavender wing against Lola's pale blue one. 'You haven't done *anything* wrong,' she said. 'Don't worry, Lola – we'll work this out and put a stop to it. It won't happen again, I promise!'

But looking at the mangled duvet again, Twink felt a cold sliver of fear. It was all very well for her to make promises . . . but, to tell the truth, she had no idea what to do.

Chapter Five

Returning to the Common Branch, Twink gathered a few of the other Peony Branch fairies around her. They huddled at the back of the branch while Twink filled them in.

Pix's face was grave. 'I'm afraid this pretty much proves my suspicions.'

'What suspicions?' asked Twink nervously. She had a feeling that whatever Pix said, she wasn't going to like it much.

Pix tapped her yellow wings together. 'Well, first of all, I've thought for some time that the culprit has to be someone from our own branch. Whoever it is just knows too much to be an outsider – where our homework is kept, whose bed is whose, and so on.'

The fairies glanced uneasily at each other. Twink's stomach lurched. Someone from their own *branch*? The thought was too awful for words!

'So,' went on Pix, 'once I started to put together all of the empirical evidence, I found –'

'Ooh, wait! I know, I know!' burst out Sili with an excited squeal. 'It's Mariella, isn't it?'

Pix looked put out. 'Well, let me explain my –'

Bimi's face was pale. 'I hate to say it, but I think Sili's right. If it's someone in our branch, then it *must* be Mariella. Because – because it all started when Lola wouldn't dance with Mariella, remember? And then today, she wouldn't show Mariella her portrait.'

Pix blinked. 'Yes, but it's not *Sili* who worked it out! I've suspected it for –'

Sooze smacked her forehead with her palm. 'Mariella! Oh, of course! And here I thought it was –' She broke off. 'Well, never mind. Sili, I bet anything that you and Bimi are right. Something's going on between those two! And Lola's things always seem to get the worst of it, don't they? *Her* peony was damaged the worst, and the torn home-work was mostly hers.'

'Yes, I was just getting to that –' started Pix.

'And don't forget the paint splashed on the beds,' put in Zena. 'Lola's bed got the worst of *that*, too. And now her duvet's been shredded! I agree with Sili. It *must* be Mariella.'

If the situation hadn't been so serious, Twink would have burst into laughter at the look on Pix's face. Instead she bit her lip, remembering Mariella's voice saying, '*Best* friends don't have secrets, Lola!' Perhaps she had decided to teach Lola a lesson . . . yet something about it didn't feel right to Twink.

'I – I don't know,' she said slowly. 'It doesn't seem very like Mariella, somehow.'

'Which part doesn't?' demanded Sooze. 'The sneaky part or the nasty one?'

Twink grimaced. 'All right, I know she's not very

nice! But still, she's never done anything like *this* before. When Mariella wants to get at someone, she – she spreads rumours, or sends anonymous notes, or –'

Sooze flapped her hand. 'So? She's branched out! Honestly, Twink, I wouldn't have thought *you'd* be on Mariella's side – the number of times she's done things to you!'

'I'm not on her *side*,' retorted Twink hotly. 'But –'

'Actually, Twink, I'm afraid it *has* to be Mariella,' put in Pix. 'I wasn't just basing my suspicions on sloppy reasoning, you know.'

'Sloppy what?' A confused frown creased Sili's forehead.

Pix ignored her. 'Hasn't anyone noticed when the pranks take place? It's always during afternoon study time – and the only one of us who's not here in the Common Branch then is Mariella! She's got that extra Creature Kindness session, and you know what Mr Woodleaf is like. If she asked to go for a drink of dew, she could be gone for ages without him even noticing!'

Twink swallowed. Pix was right: Mr Woodleaf wasn't the most observant of teachers, particularly if one of his beloved animals needed attention. It wouldn't be at all difficult for Mariella to slip back to Peony Branch during his sessions.

'Well, that proves it!' Sooze jumped up from her mushroom seat. 'I reckon we should give her a taste of her own fairy dust. Rip *her* petal duvet into pieces, and see how she likes it.'

'No!' burst out Twink. She lowered her voice. 'We can't do that, Sooze.'

'Of course not!' Bimi's cheeks were flushed with distress. 'We have to go straight to Miss Shimmery, and tell her what's going on.'

Twink hesitated, and then shook her head. 'No, I – I don't want to do that either, not just yet. She wants us to handle things on our own. She said so.'

Dropping back on to her seat, Sooze folded her arms across her chest. 'Well, what do *you* suggest, Noble Leader? Shall we just ask Mariella nicely to stop?'

Twink reddened at the sarcastic tone. Her

Opposite was great fun when it came to playing pranks, but not much help at all when it came to anything serious.

'I don't know,' she said tightly. 'If it really is Mariella, then she needs to be stopped, but – but we need to be completely sure that it's her.'

Pix shook her head. 'Twink, it *is* her. I've already explained –'

'I know!' Twink took a deep breath. 'But . . . I'm just not totally convinced.'

Oh, this was dreadful! All of her friends were staring at her in amazed disbelief. Even Bimi looked uncertain. But Twink was supposed to be in charge. She *couldn't* go along with something that she wasn't sure about, could she?

'We need proof!' she said desperately. 'And then once we have proof, we'll go to Miss Shimmery.'

'Proof?' Sooze's violet eyes began to sparkle. She glanced at Pix. 'Are you thinking what I'm thinking?'

Pix nodded, rubbing her chin. 'We'll have to set a trap for her.'

'Exactly!' Sooze shot up into the air. 'Brilliant work, Opposite! This is going to be the most glimmery fun ever – catching Mosquito Nose in the act!'

As the others burst into eager chatter, Bimi caught Twink's eye and gave her a small, sad smile. Twink smiled back, relieved that at least one fairy understood how she felt. Nothing about being in charge seemed very 'fun' to her. In fact, she thought she'd give anything at all not to be.

* * *

'Fairy Trail Powder!' announced Sooze the next morning. They were in the second-year bath branch, giving their wings a good scrubbing. 'I got a batch of it from Winn – Mosquito Nose won't stand a chance.'

Twink winced at the mention of Sooze's older sister. Somehow, things always seemed to go wrong when one of her spells or potions was involved!

'Are you sure?' she asked doubtfully. Choosing a fresh rose petal, she started to dry her arms.

Pix grinned as she wrung out her mossy sponge in the walnut bucket. 'It's perfect! All we have to do is sprinkle some on Mariella's pixie boots without her noticing, and then wherever she goes, it'll leave a trail! We'll be able to see exactly what she's been up to.'

'And the best part is, *we're* the only ones who'll be able to see the trail,' put in Sooze. 'Only fairies who know about it can see the magic.'

'But that's glimmery!' gasped Twink. 'That means all we have to do is keep putting it on her until something else happens to Lola. Then we'll know

Fairy Trail Powder

for sure if –' She broke off. Sooze was shaking her head.

'No, there's just enough for one dose. It only lasts a few hours, and Winn said this is the only batch she'll be able to do for us – she had an awful time getting hold of the mangle-weed.'

Twink frowned as she hung her petal up to dry. 'But then how will we know when to use it? We can't *predict* when the pranks will happen – if we could, we'd have stopped them before now.'

'We'll have to time it carefully, that's all,' said Pix. 'Keep an eye out, you two. If you spot Mariella and Lola quarrelling – there's our chance!'

That afternoon during Sparkle Art, Twink gazed glumly at her latest self-portrait. The Twink gazing back at her looked more worried than ever, and the badge on her chest had grown to the size of a dandelion flower. Now it read: *Peony Branch Head – Ugh!*

Mr Prism, passing by, shook his head sympathetically. 'Looks like you've got a lot on your mind.'

Twink sighed. 'I'll never get a normal-looking portrait!'

Mr Prism chuckled. '"Normal" is in the eye of the beholder, Twink. But once you feel differently about things, your portrait will look different, too.'

Like that *will really happen*, thought Twink. She couldn't imagine ever feeling differently about being in charge! She started to take her portrait down from the easel.

'No, Mariella! Stop it!'

Twink's head snapped up as she looked across to where Lola sat beside Mariella. The pointy-faced fairy was holding the moss sponge out of Lola's reach. '*Show* it to me, Lola! What are you hiding?'

'Nothing!' cried Lola. Her arms were stretched across her self-portrait, shielding it. 'It's come out wrong again, that's all – *please* let me wipe it away.'

'Girls, girls!' Mr Prism hurried to intervene as the branch fell silent. 'What's going on?'

Mariella's face reddened. She threw the sponge down. 'She won't show her painting to anyone. Not even to me – her best friend!'

'Well, that's her choice,' said Mr Prism mildly. 'Will you let *me* see your portrait, Lola? I'd like to very much, if you don't mind.'

Lola wavered, biting her lip. Finally she gave a tiny nod, and moved her arms. Spreading his wings so that no one else could see, Mr Prism gazed carefully at Lola's painting on its twiggy easel. Lola stared down at her pixie boots, avoiding Mariella's furious glare.

The Peony Branch fairies glanced at each other

with raised eyebrows. What in the world could it look like?

Even Jax, watching from the back of the branch, seemed interested. Peering quickly over her shoulder at her, Twink thought that hers was another portrait she'd love to see! But the spiky-haired fairy was no friendlier than she had been, and kept her portraits firmly tucked away in her petal bag.

'That's extremely good, Lola,' said Mr Prism finally. He smiled at her. 'Are you sure you don't want the others to see?'

Lola's thin face turned snowflake-pale. 'No – no!' she gasped.

'All right.' Mr Prism patted her shoulder. 'But I think you should save it – it's really too good to destroy.'

Cheeks blazing, Lola rolled the portrait up and shoved it away in her bag. The moment class was over, she grabbed her things and jetted from the branch like her wings were on fire. Scowling, Mariella started to follow.

'Mariella, I'd like a word, please,' called Mr Prism

from the front of the branch.

Mariella stopped short. 'But, sir –'

'Now, please.' Though Mr Prism never raised his voice, something in his tone could quell the most unruly fairy. Mariella fluttered sulkily to his desk.

Twink longed to hear what was being said, but Mr Prism was watching, waiting for everyone to leave. Reluctantly, she gathered her things together and flew from the branch behind the others.

Sooze had hung back, waiting for her. 'Today's the day, all right!' she whispered. 'Did you see? Mariella was *fuming* – she'll play another prank against Lola for sure!' Her pink wings flashed as she bounced in the air. 'Ooh, I can hardly wait to catch her in the act!'

Though Twink couldn't share Sooze's excitement, she knew the lavender-haired fairy was right. She nodded. 'We'll do it today. Do you have the Fairy Trail Powder?'

Sooze grinned and patted her petal bag. 'Right here!'

Chapter Six

Sooze drew a small acorn container out of her petal bag and took the lid off. Peering inside, Twink saw a dull yellow powder. She wrinkled her nose at it. It didn't look very magical!

'Are you sure Winn mixed it right?' she asked.

'Of course,' said Sooze, affronted. 'Her spells *always* work. Just wait, it'll be – *oof*!'

Mariella had come barrelling out of the Sparkle Art branch, and crashed straight into her. The acorn container went flying. Twink dived to save it, snatching it out of the air just in time.

Phew! she thought.

'Oh!' cried Mariella, disentangling herself with a shove. 'What are you doing hovering *here*, where anyone can fly straight into you?'

'Well, it helps to look where you're going!' said Sooze wryly. 'You're lucky you didn't get something *spilt* on you.' She gave Twink a quick look.

Twink's heart pounded as she realised what Sooze meant. Hastily, while Mariella was still glaring at Sooze, she scattered the yellow powder on to the pointy-faced fairy's pixie boots.

'Just watch where you're hovering next time!' snapped Mariella, and skimmed away up the trunk. A golden trail followed her, like a thin, sparkling ribbon.

'It worked!' gasped Twink.

'Of course it did!' said Sooze with a grin. 'Did you see her face? She won't be able to *resist* doing something to Lola during afternoon study! Ooh, I can hardly wait!'

* * *

Afternoon study had never moved so slowly before. Twink fidgeted, unable to concentrate. Finally, the magpie's call echoed through the school. At last! Shoving her things in her petal bag, Twink flitted quickly across to Pix and Sooze.

'Ready?' asked Sooze, her eyes shining.

Twink nodded. 'Come on!'

She held her breath as they flew out into the trunk. If Mariella had flown to Peony Branch, then they should see a trail of sparkling gold passing right by them, for the branch was near the very top of the school.

But there was nothing.

Sooze blinked in surprise as the three of them hovered midair, with streams of chattering fairies from different years passing by. 'But – I don't understand! I was *sure* Mosquito Nose would do something else to get at Lola today!'

Just then Bimi and the others appeared, flitting out from the Common Branch. Bimi glanced curiously at them. 'Are you coming back to Peony Branch with us, Twink?'

Twink shook her head, and watched glumly as they all skimmed away up the trunk. She was glad she hadn't said anything about the trap. It didn't seem to have been a success so far!

'Well, let's follow the trail from the start,' said Pix after a pause. 'Maybe she sneaked out of a window and doubled back to Peony Branch that way.'

The three friends plunged into a dive, weaving through the crowds of flying fairies. When they got to the Sparkle Art branch the golden trail was still there, hanging lazily in the air. A group of fourth-year fairies flew through it, oblivious to its presence.

The trail led them to the various branches where they had all had their afternoon classes, and then on to the Creature Kindness classroom, where Mariella had the extra session on her own. Twink's heart thudded as she saw that the golden ribbon went into the branch, and then out . . . and then back in again.

'She must be in there now!' she whispered. 'But look, we were right – she definitely left at some point –'

She broke off as Mariella herself came skimming

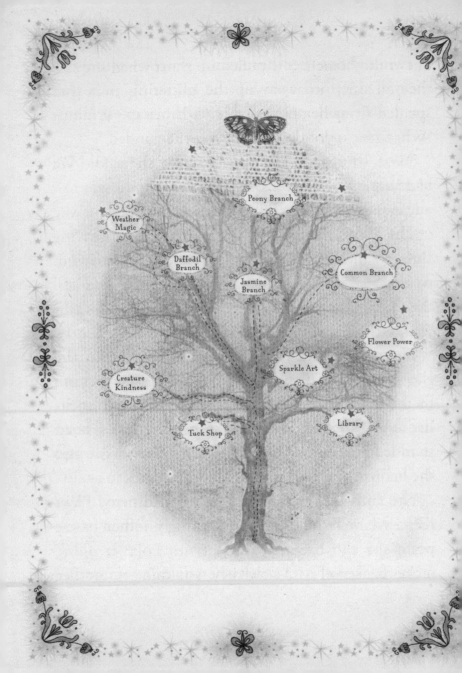

out of the branch. She pulled up short when she saw them, clearly unaware of the glittering trail that spooled from her pixie boots with her every move. 'What are *you* lot doing here?' she demanded.

Sooze shrugged. 'We missed you,' she said. 'We had to come and find you.'

'Very funny!' snapped Mariella, and zoomed away up the trunk, the golden trail sparkling after her.

Keeping out of sight of Mr Woodleaf, Twink peered quickly into the Creature Kindness branch. 'Nothing strange there,' she said. 'Come on – let's see if she went out of a window somewhere!'

The three fairies darted down the trunk. But the gleaming trail led them only to the tuck shop, and then to the fountain of fresh dew that pattered at the base of the tree. Mariella seemed to have wasted as much time as she could of her study session, but she hadn't gone to Peony Branch.

The fairies looked at each other in dismay. How could Mariella have resisted playing another prank when she had been so furious with Lola? It didn't make any sense! And now they wouldn't get another chance to follow her.

Sooze folded her arms over her chest. 'Well, I still don't see why we need *proof*. We all know she's the one who's been doing it –'

'We just do,' said Twink shortly, not wanting to start the argument again. 'We'll have to find some other way to catch her. Come on, let's get back to Peony Branch. At least nothing else has happened to Lola!'

Twink knew she was wrong the moment they flew back into their branch. Something else *had* happened to Lola. The scrawny little fairy lay huddled and sobbing on her bed. Jax sat beside her, patting her back, while Mariella stood to one side and scowled. The rest of Peony Branch hung about helplessly, looking shaken.

The torn pieces of Lola's self-portrait were scattered viciously across the floor. It looked like someone had ground a savage heel into several of the scraps, obliterating them completely.

Twink's wings turned to ice. Oh, no! It had

happened *again*. And since it couldn't have been Mariella – then *who*?

'What happened?' she asked Bimi in a low voice.

Bimi's eyes were wide and worried. 'We came here straight after study time, and found Lola's portrait like this. It *had* to have been done during afternoon study – and all of us were together in the Common Branch then! Except –' She glanced guiltily at Mariella.

'No, it wasn't her,' said Twink. She explained about the Fairy Trail Powder. 'We know exactly where she's been – she didn't come back here during study time.'

'You did *what*?' screeched Mariella. She stamped her foot, sending a flurry of golden sparks spinning about the room. 'How dare you? You think *I've* been doing these things?'

'Oh, calm down, Mosquito Nose,' said Sooze tiredly. 'We know it wasn't you now.'

'Oh! You – you – oh!' Clearly unable to think of something bad enough to call them, Mariella gave a final furious shriek and flounced from the branch, with the golden trail still swirling after her. There was a silence.

Zena looked baffled. 'But – then who could it be? Who would want to do this to Lola?'

Sooze's mouth was set in a grim line. 'I think *I* know, actually. It's what I thought right from the start. Listen, everyone. This sort of thing has never happened to us before, has it?'

Twink stared at Sooze, wondering what she was getting at. On the bed, Jax looked up, her eyes suddenly narrowed.

'I don't think –' started Pix.

Sooze held up her hand for silence. 'Think about it! We've all been together right from our first term, and nothing like this has *ever* happened. And then someone new arrives –' she pointed at Jax, 'and suddenly we're scared to come back to our branch because of what we might find!'

Twink saw Sili and Zena glance at each other, and could tell that Sooze's argument had struck a chord with them. She herself didn't know what to think. The spiky-haired fairy kept so much to herself, and was so unfriendly . . . *could* it be her?

'But Sooze, when would she have done them?' pointed out Pix. 'She's been in the Common Branch with the rest of us during the study times!'

'Yes, I'd like to hear that myself,' said Jax coolly.

Sooze flapped her wings. 'I don't know! Maybe she's picked up some tricks in one of her other schools that we don't know about – a mirror spell or something. Who knows? But it's her, I'm telling you. It must be!'

Jax stood up, her fists clenched at her sides. 'And what have I got against Lola, exactly?'

Sooze glared at her. 'Maybe you just like picking on fairies weaker than yourself. How should *I* know why you do things?'

'Well, you seem to know all the rest of it!' snapped Jax. She glanced at the others. 'What about you lot? Do *you* think I'm guilty?'

Nobody spoke. Sili and Zena stared stonily back at Jax, clearly convinced by Sooze's logic. Bimi bit her lip uncertainly, and even Pix looked torn.

'I see,' said Jax coldly. She looked at Twink. 'And

what about you?'

Twink hesitated, remembering the dance class – ages ago now, it seemed – when she had heard Jax's thoughts, and had thought that the spiky-haired fairy was sad. But Jax had been so furious when she tried to talk to her afterwards! Maybe Sooze was right.

'I – I don't know,' she said miserably. 'It *could* be

you, I suppose. But we don't have any proof –'

'Oh, you and your proof!' scoffed Sooze. 'Without Jax, there's no trouble – with Jax, trouble! What more proof do you need?'

Lola had sat up on her bed, her tear-stained face stricken. 'I – I don't think it's Jax,' she said in a small voice. 'She was really nice to me when I found my portrait torn up.'

'Yes, but she *would* be, don't you see?' said Sooze impatiently. 'She's hardly going to laugh at you and confess that it was her!'

Twink saw Lola's face turn pale, and felt a rush of pity for her. Poor Lola! The suggestion that Jax had been putting on false sympathy was obviously a dreadful one for her.

This whole situation was dreadful, in fact. And as much as Twink hated it, she knew that she was the only one who could end it.

She took a deep breath. 'Sooze, this has to stop,' she said firmly. 'We don't have any proof, and it's wrong to accuse Jax this way.'

There was a startled silence. Sili and Zena both

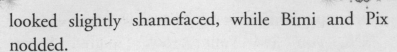

looked slightly shamefaced, while Bimi and Pix nodded.

Twink went on, not paying attention to any of them, 'And Jax, if it *is* you, then I'm warning you now: we've had enough trouble to last us a lifetime, and we're not going to put up with it any more. I'll go straight to Miss Shimmery if anything else happens, and let *her* deal with it.'

The branch was so still that you could have heard a mouse cough. Twink looked around her, meeting everyone's eyes one by one. 'Do you all understand?'

Sooze's face was poppy-red. She opened her mouth, and then snapped it shut again.

'Well done, Branch Leader,' said Pix softly. And from Bimi's shining eyes, Twink knew that her best friend felt the same.

Twink felt her shoulders straighten, as though she had suddenly grown a little bit taller. For the first time since she'd started school, she'd done something without caring what Sooze or anyone else thought of her – and it felt wonderful!

'Well, *I* understand that everyone still thinks I

might have done it,' said Jax bitterly. 'It's not over with for *me*, is it? You all still think I'm guilty.'

'We don't *know* that you are,' said Pix. 'But –'

'But you all think it, and you'll think it for as long as I'm stuck at this stupid school!' Jax scowled, her blue wings fluttering angrily. 'You want proof, Twink? Well, I think you should *have* proof.'

'What do you mean?' asked Twink in trepidation.

Jax snorted. 'Simple! It's someone from this branch, but you're all convinced that it couldn't *possibly* be one of you. Well, I'm not so sure! I say you should find out once and for all.'

'But . . . how?' Bimi's forehead was creased.

'Easy!' Jax folded her arms over her chest, challenging them all with her stare. 'Hold a fairy dust trial.'

Chapter
Seven

A fairy dust trial! Twink's wings chilled at the thought. The other fairies looked at each other uneasily. Yes, a fairy dust trial would decide the matter for good . . . but it was extremely powerful magic, normally forbidden to under age fairies . . .

Pix licked her lips. 'I – I suppose I could find the spell in the library, if I sneaked into the restricted section. What do you think, Twink? Is it a good idea?'

Everyone turned to her expectantly, waiting for her to decide. Twink swallowed, unused to being asked for her opinion in this way – but to her surprise, she found that she had an answer.

'I think we should do it,' she said softly. 'Jax is right – we *do* all suspect her. And if she's really not guilty, then someone else is. This will settle things once and for all.'

'Will we *all* have to do it?' asked Sili, her eyes wide.

Twink nodded. 'Yes, all of us – me included! It's the only way we'll ever know for sure.'

Pix looked pale, but clapped her wings together firmly. 'All right, that's decided, then. I'll find the spell and – and we'll do it tonight, after glow-worms out.'

'Wash behind your ears, you lot! Pix, get those wings polished, flitter-flutter – leaves and acorns, I've never seen such a bunch of slow-worms as you girls tonight!' Mrs Hover bustled heavily about Peony Branch as the fairies got ready for bed, *tsking* at their slowness.

Twink's arms felt heavy as she polished her wings and combed her hair. She didn't blame the others for dawdling. She wasn't looking forward to the trial, either.

In the next bed, Bimi caught Twink's eye and gave her an encouraging look. 'Don't worry,' she whispered. 'You're doing the right thing!'

Twink tried to smile, but she wasn't sure at all any more what the right thing was. But *something* had to be done – that much was certain. If only a fairy dust trial wasn't such a serious, forbidden thing!

Finally the fairies were all tucked into their mossy beds. Mrs Hover gave the branch a final scan, and nodded in satisfaction. 'Good night, my dears. Glow-worms out!'

The glow-worms in the wooden lanterns overhead put out their lights, plunging the branch into darkness. Twink lay very still under her petal duvet, listening as Mrs Hover closed the door behind her and flew away.

When she was certain that the matron was gone, Twink sat up in bed, heart pounding. 'Glow-worms on,' she whispered. 'But only one – and softly!'

A faint light lit the room. The other fairies sat up

too, looking wide-eyed and solemn. Nobody spoke.

Twink took a deep breath. 'Come on, everyone. Let's get this over with.'

The Peony fairies stood in a silent line, looking ghostly in their nightclothes in the dim light. Pix took out a bag of fairy dust – the same batch that Twink had used to play the prank on Jasmine Branch so long ago. 'I cast the spell on it earlier,' said Pix in a low voice.

Despite their gravity, fairy dust trials were simple enough: a powerful truth spell was cast on fairy dust, which was then sprinkled on someone. That fairy then had no choice but to tell the truth.

Steeling herself, Twink turned to Pix. 'Do me first,' she said firmly. 'Then I'll do you and the others.'

Pix nodded. 'All right. Stand still.'

Twink stood without moving as Pix drew a pinch of the enchanted dust from the pouch. 'Twink, are you the one who's been playing the pranks on Peony Branch?' she asked, and flung the dust over Twink's head.

The strangest sensation swept through Twink, as though the dust was worming into her mind and finding out the truth for itself. 'No, I'm not,' she heard herself say – though she herself had no control over the words.

The feeling vanished, and Twink sagged in relief. For a moment there, she had almost felt guilty! 'Jax, let's do you next,' she said. If the spiky-haired fairy *was* the culprit, it was best to get it over with quickly.

Jax flitted forward without hesitation. Twink took

the pouch from Pix and drew out a pinch of dust. 'Jax, are you the one who's been playing these pranks on Peony Branch?' she asked.

She tossed the dust over Jax's head, just as Pix had done.

It settled over Jax in a glittering cloud. There was a moment of silence as the dust did its work.

'No, I'm not,' said Jax in a slightly faraway voice.

A faint gasp of surprise rippled through the branch, and Twink let out a breath she hadn't known she was holding. So Jax really *hadn't* done it!

A moment later, Jax was herself again. 'See, I told you it wasn't me!' She folded her arms triumphantly over her chest. 'Maybe you'll think twice before accusing someone next time, Sooze.'

Sooze looked stunned, but recovered herself quickly. 'All right, I was wrong!' she said. 'But you can hardly blame me – you act like you've just sat on a nettle! And you were so secretive about that portrait of yours –'

'Sooze, it doesn't matter –' started Twink.

'You want to see my portrait?' Jax's wings flapped angrily. 'Fine! Here it is!'

Springing to her cupboard, she flung open the door and pulled out a bit of birch bark. She unrolled it with a flourish. 'There! Are you happy now?'

Twink caught her breath. Jax's portrait showed her with drooping wings and tear-filled eyes. Behind her was a series of schools, each more dismal-looking than the last. A smiling fairy couple flew away over the horizon, waving goodbye.

'Those are all the schools I've been to,' said Jax, jabbing a finger at the painting. 'And *those* are my parents. They've both got really important jobs, so I hardly ever get to see them – they just keep sending me to school after school. I've tried getting expelled so that I'll get sent home again, but it never works. They just find another new school for me!'

The fairies stared at her in horrified sympathy. Twink's throat tightened as she thought of her own loving family, always so supportive and kind. Poor Jax! How awful not to feel wanted.

'Oh, *Jax* –' started Bimi, her blue eyes bright with tears.

'Stop! I don't want you to feel sorry for me. Any of you!' Jax's chin trembled, but she lifted it proudly. 'I just thought I'd tell you, that's all. So . . . now you know.' She rolled the portrait up again and shoved it back in her cupboard.

Sooze flitted across the branch and touched her wing to Jax's. 'I really am sorry,' she said sincerely. 'I was a wasp brain. Will you forgive me, Jax?'

Surprise slackened Jax's features, and then suddenly she smiled – an open, honest smile that changed her whole appearance. 'That's all right,' she said. 'I don't really blame you – I suppose I didn't act very friendly.'

'*That's* an understatement,' laughed Sooze. The two fairies grinned at each other.

'Well, this is all very lovely,' said Mariella, tapping her wings together sourly. 'But we *still* don't know who's been doing all these pranks against Lola. It could even be Sooze, for all we know!'

Her pointed face was set in a scowl. She obviously

hadn't forgiven them for the fairy trail powder, even though it had proved her innocence.

'Mariella's right,' said Twink reluctantly. 'Get in a line, everyone. Let's get this settled once and for all.'

One by one, Twink sprinkled the others with fairy dust. Pix, Sooze, Mariella, Zena – all were innocent.

Sili was next. Twink bit her lip, unsure what to think. After Sili, only Bimi and Lola remained – and Twink knew with utter certainty that her best friend would never have played such vicious pranks. *Could* it be Sili?

If it was, Sili didn't seem worried in the least. She smiled cheerfully as Twink fumbled in her pouch for the last few pinches of fairy dust.

'This is exciting!' she said, bouncing on her toes. 'Go on, Twink, ask me!'

Twink asked the question, and threw the dust. Sili shut her eyes. 'No, it wasn't me,' she said after a moment. 'Ooh!' she squealed, her eyes flying open. 'That's *spooky*, isn't it?'

No one laughed. Bimi's face reddened as everyone

stared at her in confusion. Twink could practically
see the same thought battling in all their minds – if
only Bimi and Lola were left, then it must be Bimi
– but how *could* it be? Bimi didn't have a mean bone
in her body!

Twink looked at Lola. The scrawny fairy's face was
snowflake-pale. She stood almost shaking, staring at
the pouch of fairy dust.

Lola! The thought struck Twink like a lightning
bolt. She had found Lola alone in the branch that

day, when her petal duvet had been destroyed. And it had always been Lola's things that got the worst of it, right from the very start. Had Lola been destroying her *own* belongings? But why?

'Um – why don't you go next, Lola?' Twink tried to sound casual.

Lola gulped, quivering like a blade of grass. Slowly, Twink saw the same suspicion dawn on the faces of her friends. Sooze narrowed her eyes, while Pix's widened in sudden understanding.

'Well, *that's* hardly fair!' cried Mariella. 'Why should Lola have to go at all? It's obvious that Bimi's guilty – Twink's just trying to spare her best friend!'

'Lola?' said Twink in a soft voice. 'It *was* you, wasn't it? It was you all along.'

The thin little fairy burst into tears, covering her face with her wings. 'Yes!' she sobbed. 'Oh, please don't hate me, please don't! I just had to get away from here. I had to get away from Mariella, and it was the only way I could think of to do it!'

Chapter Eight

Mariella's face flushed an angry red. 'Get away from *me*? But I'm your best friend!'

'Well, you've a funny idea of friendship, if you ask me,' said Jax mildly. 'You're always perfectly horrid to her.'

'I am not!' insisted Mariella. 'We've been best friends for terms and terms – haven't we, Lola?' She took a menacing step forward. Lola seemed to grow smaller where she stood.

'Stop it, Mariella,' said Pix. 'Let's hear what Lola has to say.'

Lola shot a frightened glance at Mariella. Bimi rubbed her arm. 'It's all right,' she soothed. 'You can tell us.'

In short, tearful bursts, the story came out. Ever since Mariella had forced Lola to tell her the secret of fairy dust two terms ago, Lola had had misgivings about their friendship. These had become much worse the previous term, when Mariella made her take part in a cruel trick against Twink.

'I – I didn't want to,' sobbed Lola. 'But Mariella told me it was only a joke. Then when I found out it *wasn't* a joke, she threatened me. She told me I could never tell anyone, or –'

'That's a lie!' burst out Mariella, her wings shaking. 'I never forced you to do anything! Why, you should be grateful I even let you be friends with me!'

'Be quiet, Mariella,' said Sooze in a deadly calm voice. 'We're listening to Lola now. Go on, Lola.'

Lola wiped her eyes, struggling to speak. 'I tried to break things off with Mariella last term, but she wouldn't let me. She told me that I *had* to be her friend, or – or she'd turn everyone against me.'

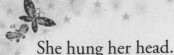

She hung her head.

Oh, poor Lola! thought Twink, her wings clammy with horror. And she herself had overheard a similar argument between them! Why hadn't she *done* anything? Shame swept over Twink as she realised the truth: she hadn't bothered because Lola was the sort of fairy you didn't really think twice about. It was like she was hardly there.

Lola took a deep breath and continued. 'I've been trying to get my mum to send me to another school for ages, but she won't do it. Then when all the pranks happened, that gave me the idea: if she thought it was *dangerous* for me to be here – if someone had it in for me – then maybe she'd let me leave.'

The branch was utterly silent. Mariella stood apart from the others, scowling. But beneath her furious expression, Twink thought she saw something else – something frightened and uncertain.

Lola swallowed hard.

'So I – I started doing all those awful pranks. I always damaged my own things worse than anyone else's, but no one really seemed to notice. So then I just destroyed my own. I thought if I kept on, then someone would tell Miss Shimmery what was happening, and then maybe she'd write to my mum and she'd come and take me away . . .'

Lola's mouth trembled. Bimi quickly put her arm around her shoulders, giving her a reassuring squeeze.

Pix's red eyebrows drew together in bewilderment. 'But Lola, how did you do it? You were always in the Common Branch with the rest of us!'

'No, I wasn't,' said Lola dismally. 'I slipped out when no one was looking. I knew no one would see that I had gone – no one ever notices me.'

The Peony Branch fairies shared a guilty glance. Lola was right, thought Twink sadly. None of them had noticed her.

'What about your self-portrait?' asked Jax. 'Why did you tear it up?'

Lola winced. 'Because it – it showed me standing up to Mariella. Like I ever really could! I *hated* it! And besides, I knew Mariella would be looking for it, and that she'd be furious if she ever saw it –

so I sneaked up here and tore it to shreds during study time.'

She wiped her eyes. 'But then when I came back to the branch and saw it all in bits like that, I started crying, and I just couldn't stop . . .' Lola trailed off, and swallowed hard. 'But Jax was so nice! She really was. She sat with me, and – and tried to help.'

Jax's cheeks turned pink with embarrassment. 'I wasn't *nice*,' she protested gruffly. 'I'm never nice!'

Mariella looked sick. 'Lola, you make out like – like I'm some sort of monster! I thought we were friends. I –' She broke off suddenly and turned away, her wings drooping.

There was an awkward silence. Lola bit her lip, clearly close to tears again.

Twink's own eyes felt hot and prickly. She cleared her throat. 'Lola, you're right. We – we haven't really paid much attention to you. But we all want to help you now, we really do! What can we do?'

The other fairies murmured assent, drawing forward.

'I – I don't know,' said Lola. 'I just wish I could

start again, somewhere where no one knows me. But my mother won't let me change schools. And I *can't* stay here, I just can't!' She shot a frightened glance at Mariella.

'*She* won't bother you again,' said Sooze grimly. 'You can count on that!'

Lola struggled to get the words out. 'Yes, but – but don't you see? It would be awful anyway, because now all of you know! Even if you pretended it didn't matter, you'd always be thinking of it – how Mariella treated me, and how I was too weak to stand up to her. I need to go somewhere new, where I can be someone different!'

The fairies exchanged troubled glances. As difficult as it was to admit, Twink knew that Lola had a point. But how could she go somewhere new when her mother wouldn't let her change schools?

'What if you changed branches?' asked Jax suddenly. 'Then you'd get your fresh start, and your mother would still be happy because you were at Glitterwings.'

Lola face creased anxiously. 'But everyone in our

year knows that I'm Mariella's friend. They don't know any of *this*, but . . . but what if they were all whispering about me? I wouldn't make any friends!'

'Well, what if I came with you?' said Jax. '*I'll* be your friend. And if anyone has anything to say about you, they can say it to me first!'

Lola gaped at the spiky-haired fairy. 'Really?' she whispered. 'You'd really do that for me?'

'Why not?' grinned Jax, flapping her wings. 'I had just about decided to stay at this miserable school anyway.'

A relieved smile burst across Lola's face. 'Oh, that would be wonderful!' she breathed.

Mariella turned slowly around again, her eyes bright with tears. 'Lola, I didn't know you felt this way,' she said stiffly. 'And of course if you *want* to go to a different branch, then I won't stop you! But – but – well, I'm sorry,' she finished awkwardly. 'I suppose – I suppose I wasn't always very nice to you.'

Lola stood very still, her eyes wide. Mariella's cheeks blazed as she looked at the others. 'In fact, I suppose

I'm not very nice at all sometimes,' she said in a low voice. 'So . . . I'd like to say sorry to all of you.'

There was a stunned silence. Twink and Bimi exchanged a look. Mariella, apologising! And for once, it sounded like she actually meant it.

Sooze flitted forward and touched Mariella's arm. 'Well done, Mosquito Nose,' she said softly. 'I think that's the most sensible thing I've ever heard you say!'

Twink cleared her throat. 'Listen, everyone, I think we should go to bed now,' she said. 'I'll go and talk to Miss Shimmery tomorrow, Lola, and see what she says about you and Jax moving branches – that is, if you're sure it's what you want.'

Lola hesitated, glancing at Mariella. 'Yes, please,' she said. 'But Mariella . . . thank you for apologising.'

Miss Shimmery sat behind her mushroom desk with her wings folded behind her back, listening carefully. She made no comment as Twink spoke, but her blue eyes looked wise and gentle. She didn't even seem cross when Twink told her about the fairy dust trial.

'You've had quite a time, haven't you?' she said when Twink had finally finished.

Twink nodded. 'It was really awful sometimes – especially when we didn't know who was playing all the pranks. And – and oh, Miss Shimmery, we were all so completely daft not to notice how unhappy Lola was!' she burst out. 'I wish that we had done something to help her.'

'Poor Lola,' said Miss Shimmery, shaking her white head. 'I, too, had no idea that she was so unhappy.' She sighed. 'Never mind, Twink. Perhaps we've both learned something, and can be more observant in future. I'm much more to blame than you are – I never imagined that something so serious might occur when I told you to handle matters on your own. I should have known better, after two hundred years of running a school for young fairies! But I think Lola will feel much happier soon.'

'Then she and Jax can move to a new branch?' asked Twink eagerly.

Miss Shimmery nodded. 'Yes, of course. And I'm delighted that Jax has decided to stay. She and Lola

may turn out to be very good for each other!'

Twink glowed happily – and then she remembered the dejected slump of Mariella's wings the night before.

'What will happen to Mariella?' she asked.

Miss Shimmery raised a white eyebrow. 'Do you have a change of residence in mind for her, as well?'

'Oh, no!' cried Twink. 'It's just – well, I know she's not very nice, but – but I think maybe she's learned her lesson this time. She thought she and Lola were friends – I don't think she really knew what a horrible bully she was being.'

Miss Shimmery opened and shut her rainbow wings. 'You may be right, Twink,' she said finally. 'But Mariella shall certainly be asked to think about what she's done, and how she can be a better fairy as a result.'

She smiled suddenly. 'And I might as well tell you, even if you *did* wish for Mariella to move branches, I would most likely say no. In her own way, Mariella is as weak a character as Lola. There are some fine fairies in Peony Branch – you set an excellent example to her, without even realising you're doing so.'

Twink stifled a giggle at the thought of Sooze setting anyone a good example! But perhaps she did help Mariella after all, by not putting up with any of the pointy-faced fairy's nonsense.

'One more thing, Twink.' Miss Shimmery's eyes were as warm as the sunshine that streamed through her window. 'You've done an excellent job as Branch Leader. I had every expectation that you would.'

Reddening from the praise, Twink blurted out the question that had bothered her from the start. 'But why did you pick *me* to do it? Why not Pix or Sooze? I could never work it out!'

Miss Shimmery chuckled. 'Couldn't you? Think about all that has happened, my dear.'

Twink thought hard, shifting on her mushroom seat – and then all at once the answer came to her. 'It's because I was so much under Sooze's thumb, wasn't it?' she said slowly. 'I didn't even know I was, but by being Branch Leader, I had to stand up to her, and – and be my own fairy a bit more.'

Miss Shimmery inclined her head in agreement.

'And I think you've learned a few things about yourself in the process, haven't you?'

'Yes, I have,' said Twink in wonder. She knew now that she could take charge if she had to, and make decisions that other fairies would respect. She'd never be swayed by Sooze again – not unless it was something that she really wanted to do!

Miss Shimmery didn't ask her to explain, but looked as if she understood all of this without Twink saying a word. 'I'm glad. You may go now, my dear. Thank you again for coming to me.'

Later that afternoon, Twink and Bimi flew through the bright summer sunshine, enjoying the tickle of wildflowers against their wings as they skimmed low across the grass. 'Oh, it's all worked out so well!' Bimi turned a joyful flip in the air. 'You must be so pleased, Twink.'

Twink grinned sheepishly. 'Yes, but you were right, you know – I should have gone to Miss Shimmery sooner.'

The two friends landed in a sunny glade. Bimi

leaned against a dandelion stalk, tipping her blue hair back. 'Well, I still think you did a good job.' Suddenly she laughed. 'But you'd better not tell Sooze that you had a chance to get rid of Mariella and didn't take it. She'd never speak to you again!'

Twink grinned at the thought, and then her smile turned wistful. She knew that something had shifted now between her and Sooze. Was she still Sooze's Opposite? Part of her hoped so . . . and part of her knew it was time to stop being Sooze's Opposite, and to just be herself.

'It's amazing about Mariella, isn't it?' said Bimi.

Twink nodded. The pointy-faced fairy had been meekly quiet all day, obviously shaken by the events of the night before. And she had gone to each fairy in the branch in turn, apologising for her past behaviour.

'Maybe she'll really change this time,' said Twink.

'Maybe,' said Bimi. 'It can't be easy for her to have apologised, anyway. I've never liked her, but you have to admire her for that!'

The two friends sat in companionable silence, stretching their wings in the sunshine. Twink watched a striped bumblebee bob past, buzzing industriously from flower to flower. It reminded her of herself, trying so hard to be a good Branch Leader. But maybe she hadn't done so badly with it after all, in the end.

'You know what?' she said suddenly. 'I'm really looking forward to our next Sparkle Art class.'

'Why's that?' asked Bimi.

Twink smiled. 'Oh, I don't know. I just have a feeling that my next self-portrait might come out a bit differently!'

The End

From New Girl

'Oh, how beautiful!' breathed Twink Flutterby.

She tipped her head back to take in the glittering crystal cavern around her. The underground room sparkled with pinks and greens and blues. It was like being inside a diamond!

'Isn't it glimmery?' said Bimi Bluebell, her best friend. 'The Crystal Caverns are my favourite place in the world. It's so great to show them to you!'

'I love them!' Twink flew to Bimi's side and squeezed her hand. 'This is the best holiday ever, Bimi.'

The two fairies smiled warmly at each other. Both were second-year students at Glitterwings Academy, and had been best friends since their very first term. Now Twink was staying with Bimi's family over the holidays, and Bimi's dad had taken them to see the famous caverns.

Titania Woods

There are lots more stories about Glitterwings Academy – make sure you haven't missed any of them!

If you have any difficulty in finding these in your local bookshop, please visit www.bloomsbury.com or call 020 7440 2475 to order direct from Bloomsbury Publishing.

Visit www.glitterwingsacademy.co.uk for more fabulous fairy fun!